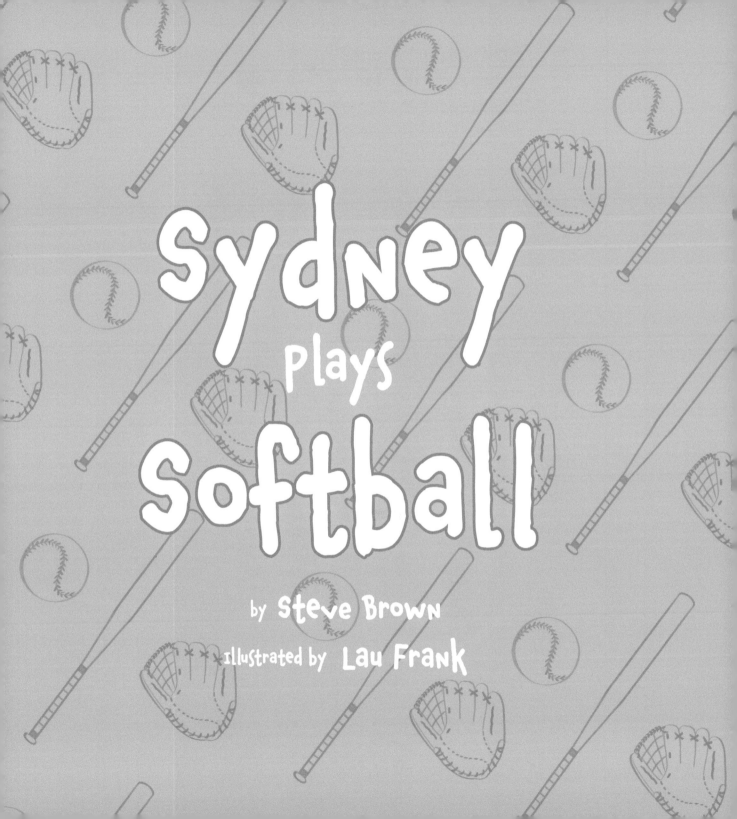

Sydney
plays
Softball

by **Steve Brown**

Illustrated by **Lau Frank**

"Steeeeeeerike one!"
"Steeeeeeerike two!"
"Steeeeeeerike three! You're out!"

"Why do only boys play baseball?" Sydney asked her dad.

"Hmmmm," he replied. "That's a great question, Sweetheart. I think it's because boys wouldn't be able to keep up with the girls if they played too."

Sydney furrowed her brow. "What do you mean, Daddy?"

"Well, girls play a much harder game. It's just like baseball, but it's called *softball*."

3

Sydney jumped up and almost dropped her cherry snow cone. "I have a softball at home!"

Well, it wasn't *really* a softball, but it was soft, and she used it mostly to play with her puppy, Bella.

4

"Would you like me to buy you a glove and ball so you could learn to play catch?" he asked.

Sydney threw her arms around her daddy and excitedly replied, "Yes, Daddy! Thank you!" Then she joked, "You're not out!"

5

Saturday mornings were the times when Sydney and her dad bought doughnuts, but when she came into the living room, it was empty.

"Daddy?" she called.

No answer.

"Daddy, where are you? I want to get my apple fritter!"

Just then, the door swung open. I wanted to be the first one in the store so I could bring this to you when you woke up!"

Sydney said, "Thanks, Daddy! This is even better than an apple fritter!"

"And you need a glove to catch the ball, so I bought you this glove too!"

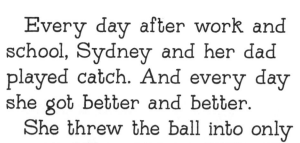

Every day after work and school, Sydney and her dad played catch. And every day she got better and better.

She threw the ball into only one window, and hit Bella only three times. But that was Bella's fault for thinking she was playing too!

8

After work one night, her dad came home
with a bat. "Today you'll learn to hit."
Sydney practiced every day with her dad
and got better and better.

One Saturday morning, on the way home from picking up apple fritters, powdered twists, and chocolate bars, Sydney and her dad saw a humongous sign announcing softball tryouts at the local park.

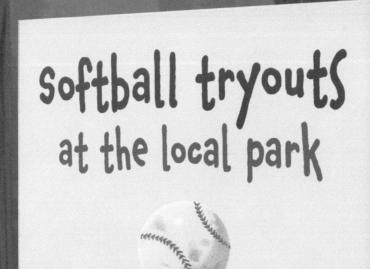

"Would you like to go to the tryouts?"
Before he could even finish his sentence,
Sydney shouted "Yes!"

For the next couple
of weeks, she practiced
harder and longer than
ever before.

The day finally arrived for softball tryouts. They pulled in to the park and Sydney shouted, "There must be a million girls here!"

While there were not quite a million, hundreds of girls of different ages showed up to hit, run, and bat in front of the coaches.

Two nights later, just after bath time, her daddy's phone rang. "Yes, of course, Coach!" he said and handed Sydney the phone. "It's for you."

"Hello?" Sydney could hardly contain her excitement.

"Sydney, this is Coach Jeff. Would you like to be on the Magical Unicorns?"

Sydney didn't have to think twice about her answer. "Yes, yes, yes, yes, yes!"

At the first Magical Unicorns practice, Coach Jeff had all the girls stand in a circle so that they could introduce themselves. "Tell everyone your name and one of your most favorite things, starting with the same letter as your name."

One by one all the girls introduced themselves.

"I'm Maddie and I like M&M's."

"I'm Lilly and I like licorice."

"I'm Jillian and I like to wear jeans."

"I'm Sydney and I like . . . softball!"

Then it was time to get to the real practice. "This area is the outfield. Each of you will have a chance to play."

After the team was introduced to the outfield it was time to learn about the infield.

"There are four bases in softball First base, second base, third base, and home plate," Coach Jeff explained as he ran to each base, stomping on each one as he arrive there.

16

After teaching the girls about the bases, Coach Jeff gathered them around a big chalk circle in the middle of the field. "This," he said, "is where the pitcher works. Some believe the pitcher is the most important player on the team!"

Then he asked, "Does anyone know who wears the most equipment on the team?"

No one answered.

"It's the catcher," he said.

Sydney had no interest in wearing all that equipment and having the ball thrown at her. Also, the other team swung their big bats very fast and close to the catcher's head!

After weeks of practice, where e girls got to try different positions d learn which ones they were tter at, opening day arrived. Everyone woke up early and t at the supermarket parking lot

to decorate the truck in pink and blue streamers for a parade, and even made the front of the truck look just like a magical unicorn!

Then it was time for the game!

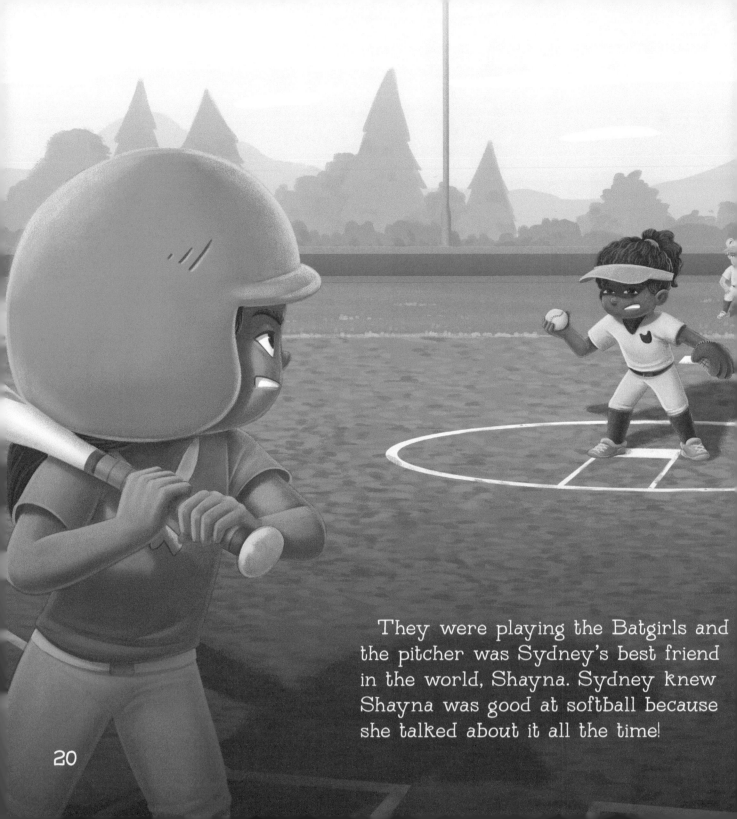

They were playing the Batgirls and the pitcher was Sydney's best friend in the world, Shayna. Sydney knew Shayna was good at softball because she talked about it all the time!

Taylor was first at bat. After three strikes, the umpire called, "Out!"
Jordan was up second. Another out!
Lauren batted third. Three outs!
Wow, that was fast, thought Sydney.

Now it was the Magical Unicorns' turn to take the field.

Maddie was the pitcher and Sydney was the catcher. Sydney decided she wasn't scared at all and just loved being part of every single play.

The first hitter on the Batgirls
it a ground ball to Amy at first
ase that went right through her
egs!

The next batter hit a pop fly
hat seemed to reach the cotton—
lled clouds in the sky.

Jillian, at third base, and Lilly,
at shortstop, both looked up to
find the ball, which seemed to
stay in the air forever. And by
the time they finished running in
circles around each other, the ball
landed right between them!

The part of the game that Sydney loved
the most were the cheers the girls sang
while their team was at bat.

"Pump, pump, pump it up! Keep that softball spirit up!"

And her favorite: "Way down deep in the softball jungle, you can hear that Paula rumble! Go, Paula, go, Paula, go!"

25

In the final inning of the game, the score was tied 9 to 9, and there were 2 outs.

Sydney's team was up, and it was her turn to bat. She wasn't nervous to make the last out of the game because Coach Jeff always said, "You play how you practice," and Sydney took practice very seriously.

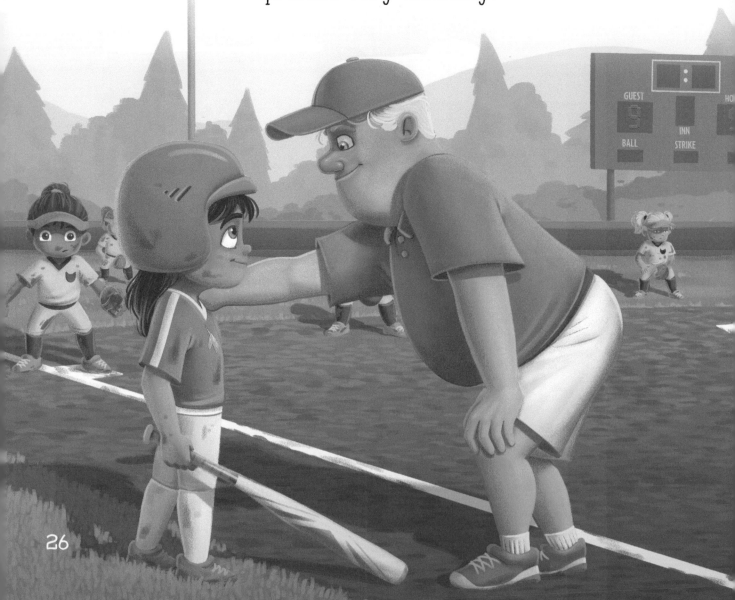

Sydney planted her feet in the batter's box and lifted the bat up above her head, ready to hit whatever came her way.

"Steeeeeeerike one!" the umpire called out.
She swung again.
"Steeeeeeerike two!"

The next pitch was faster than a bolt of lightning, but she swung with all her strength and hit it. Up, up it went, just over the shortstop's outreached glove!

As the ball bounced to the fence in the outfield, and the outfielder ran to pick it up, Sydney ran as fast as she could around all the bases. She arrived at home plate just as the ball was thrown to meet her.

Sydney slid into home plate, and in a cloud of dirt the umpire shouted, "Safe!"

Sydney hit her first home run and the Magical Unicorns won their very first game of the season!

After the game, both teams and their coaches lined up near home plate and congratulated each other with high fives!

Finally, time for snow cones.

This book is dedicated to "my" Sydney, Maddie and Shayna, whose support and love inspired me to step out of my comfort zone and fulfill a dream. I love you more than all stars in the sky... and even more than that.

Special dedication also goes out to Matt Gray and Sydney Angle, who will continue to inspire us for innings to come.

Thank you to Lau Frank for agreeing to illustrate a subject you just learned, and to dive in wholeheartedly. Your professionalism, passion, and commitment are to be rewarded!

Thank you to Bonnie Honeycutt for being the glue that brought this project from a simple idea to a complete work.

ISBN: 979-8-9860579-0-3

Printed in the United States

First Edition, April 2022

Sydney B.   Sydney A.   Maddie B.   Jillian M.   Lily P.   Amy. P

Zoe A.   Riley S.   Shayna R.   Ryan F.   Legacy M.   Sami R.

Erin R.   Skylar M.   Jadyn W.   Camryn W.   Emersyn W.   Shayna

Lightning Source UK Ltd.
Milton Keynes UK
UKHW050639170522
403108UK00008B/66